MICHAEL DAHL PRESENTS

SIDE-SPLITTING STORIES

FINDING YORGY

By Benjamin Harper
Illustrated by Christian Cornia

STONE ARCH BOOKS
a capstone imprint

Michael Dahl Presents is published by Stone Arch Books,
an imprint of Capstone.
1710 Roe Crest Drive
North Mankato, Minnesota 56003
www.capstonepub.com

Library of Congress Cataloging-in-Publication Data is available on the
Library of Congress website.
ISBN: 978-1-4965-8704-6 (library binding)
ISBN: 978-1-4965-9208-8 (paperback)
ISBN: 978-1-4965-8709-1 (eBook pdf)

Summary: In trying to earn money to attend the Monster Madness
Convention and meet their favorite movie star, Alex and Ronnie agree to
paint a neighbor's garage. The neighbor allows the boys to come into their
house for drinks and bathroom breaks. There's just one rule: don't let their
high-energy, low-obedience dog, Yorgy, out of the house. Unfortunately,
that's exactly what they do! Will the boys and their friend Kendra locate the
playful pup before it destroys the town and their chance to meet their hero?

Designer: Hilary Wacholz

Printed and bound in the United States of America.
PA100

MICHAEL
DAHL
PRESENTS

Michael Dahl has written about werewolves, magicians, and superheroes. He loves funny books, scary books, and mysterious books. Every Michael Dahl Presents book is chosen by Michael himself and written by an author he loves. The books are about favorite subjects like monster aliens, haunted houses, farting pigs, or magical powers that go haywire. Read on!

TABLE OF CONTENTS

CHAPTER ONE
TED SAVONO IS IN TOWN! . . . 9

CHAPTER TWO
PERIWINKLE BLUES 18

CHAPTER THREE
FOAMY POINTE MANOR 26

CHAPTER FOUR
YEASTY MEADOWS
AND BEYOND 36

CHAPTER FIVE
SAVERS KORNER
NIGHTMARE. 44

CHAPTER SIX
MONSTER MADNESS! 52

CHAPTER SEVEN
HOME AGAIN 59

A "LAFFY" LAUGH!

When I was in middle school, my friends recorded me laughing. (They did it in secret.) I guess my laugh sounded so goofy that it made them laugh too. My friends were pretty funny themselves. They told great jokes and hilarious stories. I wish I had written them down. But that gave me the idea to have some of my new friends write down their stories. If you feel a chuckle or a guffaw deep inside while reading, let it out. Who knows—maybe your laugh will end up in a video!

Michael Dahl

CHAPTER ONE

TED SAVONO
IS IN TOWN!

All I needed to do was make some money. Easy, right? I thought so too. But what was supposed to be my summer dream job turned into a summer NIGHTMARE.

The Monster Madness Convention was in town all weekend, and I really needed to go. Like, really-really.

"Sure," my mom said. "But you'll have to come up with the money."

I thought for a moment and then foolishly asked, "Why?"

"To buy a ticket, of course," she said flatly.

My jaw dropped to the floor. Tickets were thirty-five dollars! Where was I supposed to come up with that kind of money?

"Get a job, Alex." My dad must have read my mind. "It'll teach you responsibility."

"Can't I learn responsibility *after* the convention?" I asked.

"No," they both said at the same time. They'd been rehearsing this response, I could tell.

"Then could I get a raise in my allowance?" I asked.

"No," they both said again.

"Fine." I had no choice.

I mean, Ted Savono was at the convention. TED! SAVONO! He's the star of *Guts*, Parts One through Seven, my all-time favorite scary movies. If I missed him when he was in town, I would never—I mean, NEVER EVER—forgive myself. Ever.

My friend Ronnie was in the same boat. His parents and my parents are best friends, so I know they came up with this sinister plan together. They're probably still laughing about it right now. (Like, "BWAHAHA! Those kids'll never raise enough money! NEVVVVVVVER! BWAHAHA!")

We didn't even know where to start looking for jobs.

"Maybe mowing lawns?" I asked Ronnie as we walked through our neighborhood.

"Alex, you know I'm allergic to plants. My eyes seal shut, and I can't breathe," Ronnie moaned, scratching at his face.

"So what's the problem?" I joked.

"Very funny," he said and then added, "What about a lemonade stand?"

Gross, I thought. *No one ever stops at those.*

"I tried that once, and all I got was sunburned and covered in bugs," I told him. "Then I barfed from drinking all the lemonade that I couldn't sell. I can't even look at lemons anymore without feeling like I'm going to puke." Seriously, to this day, the color yellow makes me gag.

We were about to give up on seeing Ted Savono—TED! SAVONO!—and getting our *Guts* action figures signed. But then . . . we turned the corner and saw our neighbors, the Clambakers. With a name like that, I guess their ancestors were pretty handy with shellfish. Or maybe baking cakes. Or clam-flavored cakes . . . YUCK! I didn't want to know.

The Clambakers were busy watering their lawn and trimming their hedges. They are the nicest people ever, but then there's Yorgy. He's their little Chihuahua. Whenever I walk by their house, I can see that dog jumping up at the window, barking and spinning around so fast he's a blur.

When they take Yorgy for a walk, he pulls them so hard he's practically dragging them. (Maybe that's why Mrs. Clambaker wears those pantsuits?) Legend has it that Yorgy escaped once and ran so fast that he was in the next county in twenty minutes. That's *quick*—the next county is 53 miles away, OK?

"Yorgy, hush now!" Mr. Clambaker called toward their house. Yorgy was barking up a storm inside.

"Hello, boys," Mrs. Clambaker said, aiming the hose at a hibiscus. "My, what a nice day it is, don't you think?"

"I guess so." Ronnie slumped.

"What's the matter?" Mr. Clambaker asked.

We told them our problem, leaving out the part about *Guts*. From my experience, old people don't like *Guts*—the horror movies, or regular old guts, for that matter.

"I've got just the thing." Mr. Clambaker clapped his hands together. "What do you boys say to painting our garage? You'll make enough to get those festival tix—as you kids like to call them—and maybe even have some left over."

"Yes, sir!" we both exclaimed.

"Can you start right now?" Mr. Clambaker asked. "We need the garage in tip-top shape.

We're entering it in the local Beautiful Garage competition this summer."

"We sure can!" Ronnie said, exploding with excitement.

"Now, the trim is a lovely puce color," Mrs. Clambaker pointed to a can of muddy red paint. "And the walls should be painted periwinkle. I came up with that combination myself," she added. (I could tell.) "Over here are some old sheets if you need to cover anything up."

The Clambakers then left us to our new job and went inside. We could hear Yorgy barking at them as they closed the door.

CHAPTER TWO

PERIWINKLE BLUES

We worked all morning and didn't even break for lunch. By midday, we had more than half of the garage done. Easy money!

"Boys," Mrs. Clambaker called, "Mr. Clambaker and I have to run some errands. We'll leave the door unlocked in case you need a drink or anything, but be sure to mind Yorgy. He loves to get outside."

Oh boy, I thought. *Imagine what would happen if we let that dog out?*

Mrs. Clambaker picked up the little white dog. "Mommy wuvs her wittle Worgy Yorgy, doesn't she?" The dog licked her face so much that it was dripping. "Yorgy is her wittle baby, yes he is."

She put Yorgy inside and closed the door. She didn't even bother wiping her face as she walked to the car. Seriously, her face glistened in the sun! (Barf.)

"We'll be back in a bit," Mr. Clambaker said as they got in the car.

"Oh, and there are some ham-and-sardine sandwiches in the refrigerator," Mrs. Clambaker called from the car. "Help yourselves!" (Double barf.)

Yorgy jumped up and down in front of the window like he had a trampoline, flinging slobber against the glass. Mrs. Clambaker called out, "We wove our wittle baby Yorgy, yes we do! Mommy and Daddy wove our wittle precious!"

After they drove off, Ronnie and I got back to work. Ham-and-sardine sandwiches? No thanks!

***

On and on we painted. Periwinkle and puce. Puce and periwinkle. What a combination!

I was about to paint the next-to-last panel of puce paint when I had to go to the bathroom. I mean, bad. I guess I had been so determined to get this job done that I spaced out.

"I gotta go!" I told Ronnie as I jumped up and down. "You keep on painting the periwinkle. I'll be right back."

I ran to the door. Behind it, I heard Yorgy barking and scratching so hard that if he kept

going, he'd have dug a hole right through it.
So, so, slowly, I opened it a crack. Yorgy's little
black nose shoved right through, and he started
pushing to get out. Seriously, this dog was OUT
OF CONTROL!

I used my foot to block the door, then my
whole leg, then my body, as I slid through the
door as fast as possible. I quickly slammed it shut.

Yorgy ran in circles around my feet, jumped up
and tried to lick my face, and then ran around my
feet again. He zoomed all the way down the hall
and back. Then he did it all again. Where did this
berserk dog get his energy—from those ham-and-
sardine sandwiches?

I finally found the bathroom and shut the door.
Yorgy stood outside scratching and barking, and
scratching and barking, and then I saw his claws
scraping under the door. Then his nose. Then his
tongue!

I flushed and washed. When I turned the water off, I noticed something strange—the barking and scratching had stopped.

I opened the door. Yorgy was nowhere to be found. "Yorgy, come here, puppy," I called, but nothing happened.

And then I saw it . . . the back door was OPEN. I knew I hadn't left it that way. I wouldn't have!

"Oh no, oh no, oh no, oh no," I cried, racing from room to room. I looked under the beds, lifted couches and chairs, opened all the cabinets, dug through all the dirty laundry (remind me never to do that again), and then finally had to admit . . .

Yorgy was gone.

I ran outside and told Ronnie what happened. He was so shocked that he dropped a paint can.

SPLASH! Periwinkle paint sprayed up and covered him head to toe.

"Great, now I look like a giant blueberry," he said, wiping his hands on himself.

"Don't you mean a giant periwinkle-berry?" I laughed.

"How can you joke at a time like this? If we don't find that dog, we can forget about the Monster Madness Convention and meeting Ted Savono. TED! SAVONO!" Ronnie wailed, shaking paint from his arms.

Then he suddenly stopped and pointed. "Alex, look," he whispered. "Footprints."

Sure enough, a trail of puce and periwinkle paw prints zigzagged all the way down the Clambakers' driveway and down the sidewalk, out of sight.

I quickly locked the Clambakers' door. Then we followed those painted paw prints as they curved down the street, around the block, and right up to the entrance of . . . no, not that!

Foamy Pointe Manor.

CHAPTER THREE

FOAMY POINTE MANOR

"We can't go in there! It's haunted!" Ronnie stammered, looking up at the abandoned mansion. Every tree on the property was dead. Wind rustled through leaves on the ground and shutters flapped. He was right . . . the place was spooky.

Then, just as we were about to run away, we spotted a yapping white blur scurry up the front steps. It dashed right into the house!

BARK! BARK! BARK!

"Naturally," I said, "Yorgy has to run into the only haunted house in town."

Ronnie and I looked at each other and nodded. "OK, let's go in," we both said at the same time.

Then Ronnie jumped. "AAAAAHH!"

"Geez, it's just me." We turned and saw our friend Kendra standing behind us. "Got you good, didn't I?"

Kendra was known as the school detective. She had loved solving mysteries ever since she had cracked The Case of the Missing Fudgesicle way back in kindergarten. When we told her what was going on, she immediately offered to help.

"We'll find that dog, don't you worry," she said. She grabbed our hands and dragged us up the creaky front steps. "Come on, wimps!"

I've never been so scared in my life.

Hardly any light shined inside the house. It looked just like I imagined it would—like we were on the set of a *Guts* movie. I kept telling myself I should be enjoying this since I loved monster movies so much, but my heart wouldn't stop pounding. I was sure that vampires, ghosts, zombies, and werewolves were lurking behind every door, just waiting to eat us . . . or worse!

We heard a scratching noise upstairs. It had to be Yorgy . . . right?

Before I could blink, Kendra ran up the steps and then dashed from room to room. We chased after her, getting covered in dust and spiderwebs on the way. Yuck!

Then we came to a giant room. It was so dark that we couldn't see much. Kendra walked over to the window and pulled the curtains open with a FWOOSH! The room looked just like a vampire's crypt! (Not that I'd ever seen a vampire's crypt.)

"Oh no, a monster!" Ronnie slapped his hands to his face, screamed, and jumped five feet in the air. We turned and saw . . . a mirror.

"Wow, that's one hideous beast," Kendra joked. She pointed at the big antique mirror and then looked at Ronnie, who was now trembling in the corner. "You all need to calm down or we'll never find this dog!"

Ronnie breathed a sigh of relief. "That was a close one."

Just then, we heard more running through the house. We scampered down the stairs just in time to see a barking white blur run back outside.

As we were standing there, we heard a very *slooooow* creaking sound behind us. It was followed by a deep moan and shuffling footsteps.

We froze.

"Uh, guys?" Kendra whispered. "We need to follow that puppy outside. Like, right now."

BAM! We pulled the back door open so fast that it fell right off its hinges and onto the floor.

"Oh no," I sighed, looking beyond the crumbling porch. "Cragmire Swamp!"

Of course Yorgy had run into the swamp. Was he going to visit every spooky spot in this town? Like, what's next—the dentist's office? Now that place is creepy.

We could see him leaping through mud puddles, splashing and yapping. Every few seconds he would jump up and snap at a bug.

"Yorgy, come back here!" I called. He didn't listen. Now he was swimming through some sludge toward a bunch of trees.

"Well, let's go," Kendra snapped. We all stepped into the mud, sinking down to our knees.

Each step slurped like a suction cup as we pulled our feet out of the goo. Nasty, slimy water splashed all over our faces.

"Ted Savono had better be worth it," Ronnie said as he slapped a mosquito off his nose.

"He will be!" I said hopefully. "If we actually get to see him . . ."

Suddenly I stopped. I couldn't pull my feet out of the mud! When I tried to lift my foot, I lost my balance and fell face-first into the swamp. *Plop!*

"Hey, watch it!" Kendra yelled. "You're getting me dirty!"

"You're dirty? Look at me!" I said, scraping muck out of my eyes. I was caked from head to toe in gross, stinky mud.

YIP! YIP! YIP!

Yorgy was getting farther away! I pulled myself up from the mud, and we made our way through the trees. I got swarmed by so many gnats that it looked like a black cloud was floating around me. Some even flew up my nose! It itched so bad that I sneezed. Mud flew everywhere.

I could feel the swampy, nasty filth oozing down me as we walked. As it dried it started to crack and fall off—at least the part that was on my arms and legs. It had gotten inside my shirt and shorts too. NOT comfortable!

I stopped for a moment when we reached the edge of the swamp and scraped myself off.

Kendra pointed to a spot in the mud. Her keen eye had found Yorgy's paw prints! They led right to a hole in a chain-link fence. And that led right to . . .

Of course. Yeasty Meadows, the city dump.
Why were all these nasty places right next to each
other anyway? (Mental note to write a letter to the
mayor . . .) And why did Yorgy love these nasty
places so much?

CHAPTER FOUR

YEASTY MEADOWS AND BEYOND

Yorgy had a head start, but we saw him on the other side of the fence. He was leaping through the trash like he had hit the jackpot!

Suddenly he grabbed something out of a pile with this mouth and started thrashing it around. He was growling, and his butt was wagging back and forth. Maybe if he kept himself occupied, I could sneak up on him.

"Just hold still, Yorgy," I whispered to myself. I tried using some skills I had picked up watching Ted Savono's hit film, *Ninja Bootcamp*. I was super-stealthy, placing my feet down slowly. I didn't make a sound. My ninja skills were working! I'd have to tell Ted about it when I met him.

I was right behind Yorgy, and he was still gnawing on what smelled like a rotting fish. Even over all the other the garbage, I could pinpoint the smell of a dead fish. It was GROSS. So naturally Yorgy loved it.

I leaned over and took what was supposed to be my last step before I could grab hold of the dog when . . . *SLIP!* Whatever I stepped on sent me tumbling backward. I slid all the way down to the bottom of the trash heap.

When I stood up, I was covered in a weird gray slime that smelled a little like blue cheese. I was not happy. (I hate blue cheese.)

"Dang it, Yorgy!" I yelled at the dog. He paused to peer at us with the fish bones in his mouth. Then he turned and ran away.

"Come on!" Kendra yelled, trying to head Yorgy off at the pass. "He's getting away!"

We kept slipping and tripping on the garbage, face-first, head over heels, or falling straight down on our butts. There was just so much of it!

We rounded a giant mountain of crud and saw Yorgy. He was burrowing into a pile of what looked like old vegetables. Heads of lettuce and tomatoes were flying all over as he kicked and clawed his way in.

"You get on the right side," Ronnie suggested. "Kendra can get behind him, and I'll go to the left. If we surround Yorgy, he'll have nowhere to go!"

"Good plan," I whispered.

We tiptoed closer to him and put our plan into action. His little tail was sticking out of the garbage pile. An egg fell and splattered right on his back as he continued to dig. One thing was for sure—if we got out of this alive, we were going to need baths. And a whole bar of soap each.

Closer and closer we snuck to the pooch as he dug his way down to whatever treasure he had sniffed out in that putrid pile.

"OK, on the count of three!" I whispered. "One . . . two . . . three!"

We all jumped down, expecting to grab Yorgy. Instead, he squeezed out from behind all three of us just as the garbage mound he had been digging through gave way. We saw what he had been scratching to find: a gigantic mound of old egg cartons! We slammed face-first into them, shattering eggshells and splattering yolks and egg whites everywhere.

"I can't believe this," Kendra wheezed. She stood up, holding her arms out from her body. She was soaked in rotten eggs. We all were.

As we stood there in a daze, Yorgy dashed back over. He slurped some egg off my shoe and then zoomed off in the other direction before I could stop him.

"This just can't get any worse," Ronnie said, sitting up in his own puddle of eggs. "It just can't."

"Don't count on it," Kendra said. "Why did I ever sign up to help you find that dumb dog? Look at me! And to think I could have been solving The Mystery of the Broken Tricycle today instead." Kendra always had a backlog of mysteries she was working on.

The sun was beating down on us, and the eggs were drying. The eggs made a sort of glue that caused all the other muck on us to stick in place: lettuce leafs, coffee filters, and banana peels. We looked like walking garbage. And we stank. Bad.

YIP! YIP! BARK!

Yorgy, of course. We saw him running along the road in the dump. Every once in a while he would stop and spin around to chase his tail before plopping down and scratching behind his ears. Then he would zoom off again.

"Well, let's go." I sighed. "At least it's a clear path this time."

We chased him down the road, leaving a trail of trash behind us. When we got to the garbage dump's exit, we couldn't believe what we saw.

Yorgy had run out into the street that ran in front of the dump. All the cars had slammed on their brakes. Tires screeched and people were rolling down their windows to yell.

"You dumb dog!" a lady shouted from her SUV. I had to agree with her. Yorgy was a dumb dog. But he was a dumb dog that I needed to catch— and fast. What if the Clambakers were already home and saw that not only was the garage not done, but that we had run off . . . and so had their little Worgy Yorgy? We would be in epic trouble.

We crossed at the crosswalk when the signal changed to WALK.

"What happened to you kids?" someone called from his car. "You look like garbage zombies!"

When we got across the street, we saw where Yorgy had run to. Naturally, it was the Savers Korner Outlet Mall.

CHAPTER FIVE

SAVERS KORNER NIGHTMARE

"Ew, what's that smell?"

We had crossed the street and, against our
better judgment, entered the madness of the outlet
mall parking lot. Since it was a Saturday, the place
was packed with shoppers, all rushing around
trying to find super bargains. And to make matters
worse, a big banner at the entrance of the outdoor
mall read:

"SUPER SAVINGS SATURDAY! 75% OFF EVERYTHING!"

I think almost everyone in town was at the mall. We could barely move through the crowds, but suddenly a funny thing happened. The crowds parted, everyone holding their noses or running away from us, screaming.

"Gee, what's with these guys?" Ronnie said. I guess he forgot that we had just run through a cobwebby haunted house, a stinky swamp, and a garbage dump.

"Earth paging Ronnie," Kendra joked, pretending to talk into a walkie-talkie.

Suddenly we stopped. We were in front of Mirror Mania, the go-to place for any of your reflective needs, and our images were way worse than we had expected. We were brown and green and blue from head to toe, with bits of stray

garbage plastered to us. We looked like Bigfoot would if he had rolled in honey, then taken a bath in a tar pit, then gone dumpster diving. The three of us were terrifying. And totally rank.

"Oh wow," I gasped, looking down at my clothes. I had never been so embarrassed in my entire life.

"Alex?" I heard a familiar voice say.

Remember when I said I had never been so embarrassed in my entire life? Well, I immediately broke that record and became even *more* embarrassed. Because now I was standing face-to-face with Fanny Farnsworth. Yes, *the* Fanny Farnsworth, the most popular, perfect girl in my grade. Wait, in the entire school.

Fanny was pinching her nostrils closed and looking like she might need one of those motion-sickness bags they have on airplanes. Her friend

Gladys Greystone was fanning her hand in front of her face, and another girl I didn't recognize looked like she was choking.

"You three STINK!" Fanny shrieked. They all pointed in horror.

"Run for it!" I shouted to Kendra and Ronnie. We turned and sprinted, running anywhere to get away from those girls. All I needed was for them to go to school in the fall and tell everyone how I had been waddling around at the mall caked in biohazard. My only hope was that she didn't recognize us under all this gunk.

ARF! ARF! BARK!

We stopped cold. There was Yorgy!

I tiptoed over to him. He was sniffing around the fire hydrant. He was so busy that he didn't realize I was right behind him. I bent over and was about to grab him when . . .

"Oh no!" Ronnie screamed, diving next to me. "It's the Clambakers!"

Sure enough, the Clambakers were right inside the Cram-N-Carry Bulk Goods store, standing at the checkout. They were buying three shopping carts full of dog food, dog toys, and flea-bath products. And if I didn't catch this dumb dog, they'd be stuck with it for a long time.

Ronnie's scream had startled Yorgy out of his sniffing frenzy, and the little monster had run off again. I scanned the crowds.

"He's over there!" Kendra jumped up and down, pointing toward the Frankophile Hot Dog Cart.

Yorgy had stopped running and was circling the kid working there, barking and jumping up. It seemed he liked hot dogs even more than rotten fish.

"Get away from me, you little mutt!" the kid shouted, trying not to drop the chili-cheddar frankfurter he was making. "I'll call animal control, and then you'll be sorry!"

"Oh, don't be so mean to that little angel," cooed the lady who had ordered the hot dog. She bent over and patted Yorgy on the head. "You want a wittle bite of hot dog, puppy?"

She broke off a chunk of her all-beef frank, and Yorgy wolfed it down like he hadn't eaten for a week. He begged for more, but the lady was starting to walk away.

Yorgy ran after her, and we ran after him. But we were too late . . .

He had followed her onto a bus, which read: **EXPRESS BUS TO DEL BROOK CONVENTION CENTER**

We all pounded against the bus's door, leaving grimy brown handprints on it as it drove away. Defeated, we watched it go. As the bus zoomed into the distance, Yorgy peeked out the rear window. He was hopping up and down like crazy. Was he laughing at us?

CHAPTER SIX

MONSTER MADNESS!

The Del Brook Convention Center was only two blocks away. If we ran, we could get there pretty soon after that bus.

"This is out of control," Kendra wheezed. Clumps of garbage littered off of us as we jogged down the street. We probably left a smelly cloud of fumes in our wake.

"There it is!" Ronnie pointed. Sure enough, the bus had just unloaded its passengers and was turning back toward the mall. We watched as it drove past. It was completely empty. Yorgy must have gone into the convention center.

"We'll never find him now." I slumped down on the side of the road. My goal of meeting Ted Savono—TED! SAVONO!—had been dashed to bits by a hyper dog. How would I ever get the money? The Clambakers would probably never speak to me again!

At that moment, a group of people dressed like zombies shuffled by. They were on their way to the Monster Madness Convention.

"I've got an idea!" Kendra shouted, jumping up. "Follow me, and we'll get that dog back."

Quick as a flash, she got behind the shuffling zombies. She dragged one foot behind her like any good undead creature would, waving for us to join her.

"Let's go!" I said to Ronnie. We ran over and joined the zombies. I hoped we didn't smell too bad. A lot of the crust had fallen off, but we were still super gross.

We got to the entrance of the convention center and were in line to get in. We huddled as close as we could to the zombies.

"Go on through," the bored security guard said. "Head over to the costume contest, straight through there." She pointed to an area behind a curtain, where we saw people dressed like all sorts of monsters and ghosts.

"Wow," Ronnie sighed. "I can't believe it. We're actually here!"

"Yeah, but we don't have time to enjoy ourselves," I reminded him. "We've got to get that dog. Maybe we'll still be able to come back tomorrow if we finish painting."

A hand grabbed us.

Suddenly, we were all pulled through a curtain and onto a giant stage!

"And now, ladies and gentlemen, here we have the winners of today's cosplay competition, the Westwood Zombies!"

Applause shook the convention center.

And . . . Ted Savono came onstage. TED! SAVONO!

"For winning first place, I award you this Golden Werewolf!" He handed the statue to the head zombie. I couldn't believe it. I was onstage with the one and only Ted Savono! I was so excited I almost peed.

"What's that smell?" he asked as he walked past us toward backstage. Ugh, thank goodness we were unrecognizable.

"Hey, over there!" Ronnie pointed, snapping me out of my starstruck haze. "It's Yorgy!"

"OK, you guys, this is our last chance," I said. "We've got to surround him and grab him!"

Yorgy was very focused on the snack bar. The nacho cheese bucket was dripping molten, golden goodness onto the floor. He licked up the ooey-gooey deliciousness as soon as it landed. His little tail wagged wildly.

Kendra raced around behind the other contestants. Ronnie and I split up and snuck up behind Yorgy from opposite directions.

That cheese just kept leaking onto the floor, and Yorgy just kept licking it up.

He didn't even notice when I jumped behind him and grabbed him! He just licked, licked, licked. A small puddle had formed from all his slobber.

"Gotcha!" I shouted victoriously as I picked him up. He started scrambling so frantically that I thought I would drop him. "What am I gonna do? He's kicking like crazy!"

"I know," Kendra said. She grabbed a French fry carton out of the garbage and filled it up with nacho cheese. "This'll keep him occupied while we get him home."

We ran out of the convention center with Yorgy's face burrowed into the French fry box.

"It's stuck on his head." Ronnie laughed.

"Just what he deserves," I said as we raced down the street. "Besides, he likes it that way."

But then I froze. Right next to us at the stoplight were . . . yep, the Clambakers.

CHAPTER SEVEN

HOME AGAIN

"Oh no," Ronnie said. Yorgy was flipping back and forth, trying to get away since he had eaten all the cheese. But I held fast. Cheese and slobber oozed down my arms. "We are going to get in so much trouble!"

We jumped behind a hedge and watched as the Clambakers pulled into the post office. Mr. and Mrs. Clambaker got a bunch of boxes out of the trunk of their car and carried them inside.

"Now's our chance! They'll be in there a while," Kendra ordered. "Run!"

We leaped into action and raced down the street as fast as we possibly could. Yorgy was yapping and fidgeting and flinging cheese drool everywhere. But there was no way I was letting go of that dog until he was safe inside his own home.

We rounded the corner and got to the Clambakers' just in the nick of time. They hadn't gotten home yet!

"Ronnie, you get back to painting! We still have to finish this garage!" I said, pointing to the almost-completed project.

"I'll help," Kendra offered. She was a good detective and a good friend. "After all this, I can't let you fail now!"

I carried Yorgy up the steps and was about to open the door to let him in when I heard barking . . . from INSIDE THE HOUSE. Barking?

I opened the door . . . and there was . . . Yorgy? YORGY! He had been here the whole time! But I had looked everywhere!

"Wait a minute," I said. "If you're in there, then WHO is this?!?"

I pulled the cheese box off the impostor dog's head. The orange goo had slicked back this poor pooch's hair, and it looked like he was wearing an orange helmet.

I looked at the tag.

"MY NAME IS KIPPERS. IF FOUND, PLEASE CALL TED SAVONO."

NO. WAY.

I slumped behind the door. Both dogs jumped up on me and started licking my face. They wouldn't get off me. Cheesy dog breath. Gross!

I called the number on Kippers' tag, and can you believe it? TED! SAVONO! answered!

"Uh, I'm Alex. I've got your dog, Kippers," I told him.

***

I carried Kippers over to Kendra and Ronnie.

"You're not going to believe this," I said, holding Kippers out to them. "This is not Yorgy."

"Real funny, Alex," Ronnie said.

"No joke," I said. "But we can't worry about it now. We've got to finish this garage. First, though, come over here."

Kendra and Ronnie followed me to the side of the Clambakers' house, where I sprayed them down with the hose. Brown sludge ran off them as they turned and made sure I got it all.

"My turn!" I said. So Ronnie hosed all the gunk off me.

"Hold this dog still while I de-cheese him," I said. I gently washing all the crud out of NOT-Yorgy's fur.

Then we got back to painting. We finished the garage just as the Clambakers pulled back into the driveway.

"Looks nice, boys!" Mr. Clambaker said, admiring our work. "And who's your friend?" I was introducing Kendra when a giant limousine pulled up to the curb. The door opened and out stepped Ted Savono.

TED! SAVONO!

"I can't thank you enough for finding my little Kippers," he said, shaking our hands. "He's been missing ever since I got into town yesterday!"

"Why, that looks just like my Yorgy!" Mrs. Clambaker exclaimed, noticing Kippers, who was tied to the tree with Yorgy's spare leash.

"I'll say it does," Kendra added, glaring at me. She looked like she was going to explode.

"Here," Ted Savono said, handing us each a plastic-coated badge. "I've got these guest passes for the Monster Madness Convention. Why don't you all come tomorrow as my guests?"

"Thanks!" we all exclaimed. Maybe it hadn't been such an awful day after all.

Mr. Savono scooped up Kippers and got back into his limo. We all waved at him as he drove off.

"Nice work, boys!" Mr. Clambaker said, pulling out his wallet. Now we'd have some spending money for the convention too!

"I'll get us some ham-and-sardine sandwiches to celebrate what a fine job you did on our garage," Mrs. Clambaker said, clapping her hands together. "I'll be right back!"

And when she opened her door, Yorgy jumped out and raced down the street.

"Not again!" we all groaned.

"Again . . . ?" Mrs. Clambaker asked.

GLOSSARY

allowance (uh-LOU-uhnss)—money given to someone regularly for jobs or tasks

Chihuahua (cheh-WAH-wah)—any of a breed of very small large-eared dogs that originated in Mexico

cosplay (KAZ-play)—the practice of dressing up as a character from a work of fiction, such as a comic book, video game, or TV show

errands (ER-uhnds)—a short trip taken to do or get something, especially for someone else

frankfurter (FRANK-fuhr-ter)—another word for hot dog or sausage

keen (KEEN)—able to notice things easily

periwinkle (PER-ee-win-kuhl)—a light purplish blue color

puce (PY00S)—a brownish-red color

DISCUSSION QUESTIONS

1. What was Alex saving money for? Have you ever saved money for something important to you? What did you do to earn the money, and was it worth it?

2. Think of a time you were asked to be responsible for something. How did you handle the situation? Did you keep your cool or freak out?

3. What happened when Alex and his friends ran into Fanny Farnsworth at the mall? What was the most embarrassed you've ever been? How did you react? Thinking back, is there a way you could have handled the situation differently that might have made it better?

WRITING PROMPTS

1. Is there really any such thing as "the most popular, perfect person" at your school? Now think about the nicest person in your school. Is it the same person? If not, make a list of the ways they are different. Decide which qualities are more important to you.

2. Have you ever experienced a case of mistaken identity? Draw of a comic strip of that situation or a funny situation of identity mix-up that you create.

3. Write a paragraph about all the things the real Yorgy might have been doing at home while Alex and his friends were chasing Kipper. Did Yorgy have an adventure of his own?

ABOUT THE AUTHOR

BENJAMIN HARPER has worked as an editor at Lucasfilm LTD. and DC Comics. He currently works at Warner Bros. Consumer Products in Burbank, California. He has written many books, including *Obsessed With Star Wars* and *Thank You, Superman!*

ABOUT THE ILLUSTRATOR

CHRISTIAN CORNIA was born in Modena, Italy. He attended the School of Comics "Nuova Eloise" in Bologna. Christian has created artwork and characters for advertisements, publishers, , video games, and role-playing games. He has worked as a colorist and as an inker for Marvel USA on comics that included Ironman, The Avengers, and Daken. In 2011, along with other Italian artists, Christian founded the cultural association Dr.INK, which self-produces illustrated books.

JOKING AROUND

What do little dogs like for dessert?
Pupcakes

What dog goes "Tick-tock, tick-tock?"
A watch dog

How is a dog different from a marine biologist?
One wags a tail and the other tags a whale

How is a dog a lot like your phone?
They both have "collar" ID.

What kind of dog would you find in a desert?
A hot dog

What kind of dog always sneezes?
Achoo-wawa

What should you do if your dog starts chewing this book?
Take the words right out of its mouth.

What do you call a dog who does magic?
A labra-cadabra-dor!

MICHAEL
DAHL
PRESENTS

FOR MORE HILARIOUS STORIES, CHECK OUT

GROSS GODS

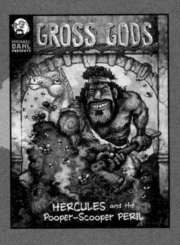

HERCULES and the
Pooper-Scooper PERIL

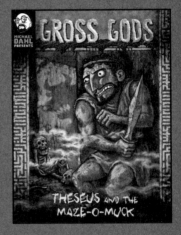

THESEUS and the
MAZE-O-MUCK

MEDUSA and Her
Oh-So Stinky Snakes

JASON and the Totally FUNKY FLEECE